Old Guys Playing Golf

Tom Manchester

ISBN: 979-8-89175-178-1 (sc)
ISBN: 979-8-89175-180-4 (hc)
ISBN: 979-8-89175-179-8 (ebk)

Foreword

I started playing golf around age 30 when a buddy at work invited me to join him. Up until then I was a golf-snob, thinking of it as a dull pastime for those who didn't have the balls to do something exciting like motorcycle racing. Motorcycle racing was what I had been doing and it was exciting. And like many such exciting pastimes it was also dangerous and a crash resulting in several broken bones, including a smashed left tibia put an end to that career. After nine months of healing, I began to think that golf might not be such a bad idea after all. I had always been good at eye-hand coordination skills. Maybe I could be good at this!

Of course I had no idea what I was getting into. My buddy tried to coach me, but he was not a professional golf instructor by any means so I was mostly left to figure out how to do this by trial and error. We were in Northern Virginia at the time, and there were some beautiful Fairfax County public courses that you could play for a very reasonable price. I bought a set of Jack Nicklaus Golden Bear golf clubs and went about learning to play golf on my own. I got a great teaching job at Northern Virginia Community College where I mostly worked in the evenings, so I could play three times a week when the weather was agreeable. I got to where I could shoot in the mid-80s consistently.

Then I got a serious job and a serious career. The opportunities to play golf seriously diminished as well.

Then I retired…

Old Guys Playing Golf

We do this for fun, right?

This particular question first came up during a round in Sedona, AZ on my wife's work boondoggle. I was partnered with her colleague Warren, a great guy and a good golfer (At the time. He's still a great guy, but at 82 he has given up golf.) And the course was beautiful…that is until it began to rain. A light drizzle slowly turned into real rain, and we were getting to be thoroughly soaked and cold. We were huddling in the golf cart contemplating our tee shots on #9 when we turned to each other and questioned our mutual sanity in continuing the round. We agreed that a hot shower and some dry clothes sounded like a much better idea! Perhaps followed by a libation in the bar by the fireplace…

So why do we keep doing it?

I remember a placard from one of my first jobs that said: "It takes 5 attaboys to make up for one aww-shit." Well, golf seems to work the other way around. One really beautiful shot can make up for several dubs, hooks, shanks and slices and make it all seem worthwhile.

Ruthlessness

Then there is the ruthlessness of the scorecard. One time I lined up my shot. I was under a pine tree with about 30 yards to the green, which was elevated. I chose a 5 iron, choked way up on it and played the ball well back in my stance so it would come off low, hit the embankment and pop up onto the green with most of the energy absorbed by the grassy embankment. I executed it beautifully, but it hit a duck (really!) and landed in a muddy, unplayable lie. The duck limped away. I don't think I caused any permanent injury…

Then there was the shot that landed a foot short of the green and rolled back down the hill to rest right by my feet… no need to change clubs, I guess.

On the other hand, there was the 120-yard dub that hit the pin and fell into the hole. The scorecard just records strokes. It has no place for style-points!

Play nicely with others

It's nice to play with friends, or friendly people with whom you can share the joy of everyone's (anyone's) success. I have played golf with a lot of complete strangers, and I can think of a couple of occasions where they were sort of assholes, but on the zillion other times they were always nice people…. sometimes very interesting, nice people!

I was playing with a complete stranger at the La Quinta Mountain course recently… long Par 5, we are both on the green, him away by 10 feet or so and on the same line as me. However, he was lying 2 and putting for eagle. I was lying 5 and hoping for bogie. He started to line up his putt when I interrupted and pointed out that my putt is on his line, and since he is the one putting for eagle, he should watch my putt and not the other way around. I promised that if I ever end up with an eagle putt (never happened) I would ask for the same courtesy. I aimed straight for the cup so he could see the how the ball would break. Didn't quite sink it, but he got a good lesson. He missed eagle by a couple of inches, but we still celebrated his birdie on a 560-yard par 5!

Warren and I played at the Marriott Desert Springs course on another of my wife's work boondoggles. It was a scrambles tournament, and we were put into a foursome that included a fairly ordinary golfer (like me) and a big guy who could absolutely crush the ball. If it happened to go straight (no guarantee) it was magnificent! However, neighboring houses were definitely in danger. So, we came up with a strategy where Warren, "Mr. Consistent," would hit a clean shot into the fairway. Then Igor (don't remember his real name) could swing away, for better or for worse. The other two of us would do our best, but we rarely hit best ball off the tee. However, there was a rule that you had to use at least two tee-shots from each player, so if either of us hit a pretty decent shot, we would use it. My buddy had a couple of good tee-shots, but I was struggling from the tee. We came up to a 120-yard par 3 that had the green on an island with about 50 yards of water in between. I dubbed my shot with enough topspin that it skipped twice on the water, hit the embankment and popped up onto the green (Jesus' walk-on-water-shot). I was closest to the pin! Anyway, my short game was working well, so I pulled my weight for the round, and we ended up 8 under par and won the tournament! We each got shirts with the hotel logo hummingbird on it. I wore it until it finally fell apart (did I tell you how I got this shirt????).

Back to Old Guys Playing Golf

I've since retired and play golf twice a week with some buddies. Somehow, we all became "old guys playing golf." I said it to myself and didn't like the sound of it, but I've learned that there are some good things about being old guys playing golf. We have some gentlemen's' agreements:

1. No score higher than a 6 (it's a par 3 course)
2. Any putt shorter than a putter length is a "gimme[1]"
3. (Covid when there were no rakes allowed) free drops from sand traps[2]
4. No 3-putts when the greens are aerated and covered in sand

---

[1] The putter length can be a variable. The true standard is Ray's putter since he is the arbiter of all things, but if there is a twosome behind us making us need to hurry up, the putter length can become a little longer by general consensus.

[2] They have put the rakes back so we no longer have an excuse for the free drop. But our sand skills are improving…

5. A score lower than 40 (9 holes) is officially a good score

Ray is a retired district attorney. We ask him for rulings on these matters. We may as well ask him because he'll make them anyway! He does some classic "old guy" things:

1. He hits his driver any time the distance is over 100 yards
2. He hits his putter any time he is within 50 yards of the green
3. He never tries to hit over a hazard, but "triangulates" his way around it
4. He executes those shots amazingly well!

Ray putting from off the green

Ron was HUD Housing Rehabilitation Contractor. He can't see worth a damn and always asks us where the pin placement is. He often hits the best tee shots, and I believe it is because he has no reason at all to look up from the ball… he can't see anything anyway! When his game is on, he is really good. I think the lesson is that vision is overrated, at least as far as golf goes.

Gary was/is an engineer[3]. He understands the mechanics of the game quite well, but like the rest of us, doesn't manage to execute that understanding into prefect shots quite every time…. sometimes, but not every time.

Me, I'm a jack of all trades (master of none?) but I always enjoyed learning things and I find golf to be a never-ending opportunity. I've played off-and-on for much of my life. You know how they say that some things are like riding a bicycle…. once you learn to do it, you never forget? Well golf is NOT like riding a bicycle! You can be pretty good at it, lay off for a while, then come back to find that you completely suck again! It's a sort of kinesthetic Alzheimer's where you execute perfectly one day, only to find that you are a complete klutz the next (or even from one hole to the next). So, the learning, and the need for it, never stops. My wife has occasionally asked me if she should take up golf. My response is: "Well, do you feel as though you don't have enough frustration in your life, and you need some more? Then take up golf."

---

[3] There are professions, and then there is being an engineer. An engineer IS an engineer. He/she can't help being one. They can retire from the profession, but they can never stop being one.

But it's rare for us all to suck on any given day, so we try to find some joy in at least one of us playing well. It's even more rare for us all to be on top of our games on the same day, but we do occasionally play "best ball," which averages out our "suck vs genius" ratio into a score of which we can all be proud, even though it doesn't really mean anything…

The Golf Course

We play The Links at Bella Mare Resort, which is a beautiful location with expansive views along the Palos Verdes Peninsula coastline and of Catalina Island, 26 miles across the Pacific Ocean. The course is well maintained and might look easy to the untrained eye. Are you familiar with the word "barranca?" It refers to the coastal scrub undergrowth that is native to southern California and is carefully maintained by dedicated environmentalists in a manner that guarantees that if your ball goes into it, you will not find it. Strangely, you can almost always find other balls that have been abandoned by other frustrated golfers, but not your own. There is some kind of natural rotation cycle at work whereby a newly devoured golf ball remains hidden for about two weeks, before being released back into the environment. I hypothesize a two-week cycle because on the 6th hole I lost a ball into the barranca on the left (a severely hooked shot) that was a distinctive ball with an Acura logo on it (I got them free at work). All four of us tried to find it without success. Two weeks later, I hit a similar shot with a completely different ball. It, again, was lost, but I found my Acura ball from two weeks ago! Unfortunately, I've been hitting much straighter shots on that hole since then (or shanking it right), so I haven't been able to prove my 2-week hypothesis.

Besides the barranca, the course is also liberally dotted with sand traps. It's funny how course designers seem to know where the average Joe is going to hit the ball. And instead of doing the nice thing and putting the hole there, they put a sand trap there.

The Bella Mare sand traps can be pretty cavernous, but they are also surrounded by "bear grass." I call it that because it reminds me of a long, fibrous grass that florists like to use in flower arrangements. If your ball gets stuck in the bear grass you will have a difficult time getting your club face to make contact with the ball, and you will probably be standing with one foot three feet below the other, trying to find some footing in the sand so you don't fall over as you swing. This sometimes results in a very embarrassing whiff.

With the inception of COVID rules and the elimination of sand trap rakes, we awarded ourselves free drops out of the sand. This was purely for the sake of maintaining the condition and esthetic value of the sand traps, of course. Never mind the strokes we happened to save in the process. When one of us hit a shot that was heading for a trap, we would hope that it went in and NOT get stuck in the surrounding bear grass, which was not eligible for a free drop (according to Ray's interpretation of the rule, which we made up ourselves anyway).

Ray is handy to have around for such matters. For instance, the question often comes up as to whether a swing was a whiff, or just a practice swing. Ray's answer is simple: it is a matter of intent. If it can be established that the golfer intended to hit the ball with that swing, then it is a whiff and counts as a stroke. If there's a hung jury, then it is down to the honesty of the golfer.

Anyway, Bella Mare is deceivingly beautiful and offers lots of opportunity for small mistakes to turn into lost balls, unplayable lies or really difficult shots. Even if you hit your tee shot onto the green, you still may have a challenge getting down in two. There is a phenomenon found on many golf courses that are near the ocean that makes the ball break in a manner that is very difficult to read. We say that the ocean "sucks" because the ball tends to break toward it, sometimes in defiance of the apparent slope of the green. And since Bella Mare is on a peninsula, there may be ocean on multiple sides of the green. In short, shooting a good round is a challenge and is very gratifying when you manage to do it.

Ray is also known as "The Finnish Retriever" because his ancestry is from Finland and he is very good at finding errant shots. Once he gets off the course looking for golf balls, we may not see him for a while. Sometimes the rest of us resume play and hope that he'll catch up before the next tee.

The Finnish Retriever

Addressing the Ball

We each have our routines for "addressing the ball.[4]" Ray is always the most studied. He puts the tee into the ground, then carefully assesses its height. Then he places the ball on the tee and rotates it to get the right part of the ball oriented to the club. Then he takes his stance and aligns the club to

---

[4]   The term makes it sound as though we are either putting the ball into the postal system to send it somewhere, or speaking to it as a person to whom we wish to respectfully communicate! I often speak to my ball, trying to reach a mutual understanding of what I expect it to do! However, golf balls are a lot like children, they just don't listen to instructions!

the ball. Inevitably, he readjusts the tee height and checks again. Then he steps back and takes three practice swings. Then he steps up to the ball, takes a look toward the green, looks for all the world as though he is actually going to hit the damn thing, but he almost always steps back and takes two more practice swings. Sometimes he does that routine one more time before actually hitting it. Sadly, none of that guarantees the result. Like the rest of us, he hits some damn fine shots and he hits some dogs.

Ron, the Cyclops

Ron is sometimes known as "The Cyclops" because he can barely see out of one of his eyes and can't see at all out of the other. He starts his tee shot by asking us where the pin is (he can't see it), then he carefully makes a line in the grass next to the ball with his club so he can align his feet in the right direction. Then he takes three practice swings. His form is pretty good for an old guy, head stationary and swing rotating around his backbone, left arm straight…slow and deliberate… I always worry that he is using up perfectly good swings with his practice swings. Sometimes I am right. Other times he hits a damn-near perfect shot. Hey, if we were perfect all the time we'd be pros, right?

Gary's 90 degree elbow backswing

Gary is methodical, but gets it all done a lot more quickly, time being a commodity that an engineer would never waste. Gary is all about the backswing. He rotates his body and wraps both arms all the way around his neck. When he connects it works amazingly well. Other times.... well, he needs the Finnish Retriever to help.

Me, I worry that I only have so many good swings in me, and I don't want to waste one on practice. I tee my ball very low, or on the grass if it is in good condition, then put another tee in front of the ball pointing toward the pin. The theory is that it will help keep me from looking up, and if I focus on sweeping up that tee with my club, I will hit through the ball and make good, clean contact with the sweet spot of the club. Then I get my grip right, which is a technical thing and never feels quite normal. I'm a mechanic, among other things, and I know how to hold a hammer or a wrench. That feels quite normal. If you hold a golf club the same way, it doesn't work. So, I hold it as I'm supposed to, thumb and forefinger angles aligned, right hand wrapped around the top...I don't think it will ever feel normal. I take some air swings to loosen up, then address the ball, near my right foot for a short iron, closer to the left foot for longer irons. Then comes my peculiar stuff...my left leg is shorter than my right leg and it's a little bit crooked (another story!) and so my natural stance is leaned to the left.... the wrong way. My golf teacher, Daryl (great guy) looked at this and taught me to get myself lined up, then lean right until my eyes are over the ball. Now I'm crooked. So, I have to rotate my hips clockwise to get square again. Now I'm all wound up and ready. Slow backswing, left arm straight, focus on scooping up the alignment tee and following through. Sometimes it works perfectly! Other times…well. At least my bad shots are usually playable these days, many thanks to Daryl!

Trying to swing without falling over

People talk about an ideal golf swing being smooth and natural, and you watch a pro and it looks smooth and natural. Then you try to do it yourself…nothing natural about it. A sledge hammer swing feels more natural. I love my pitching wedge. It's good to have confidence in a club, and I have this ancient Jack Nicklaus Golden Bear PW that says to me that we can make this shot! I have another, more modern pitching wedge that is counterweighted, bottom weighted, perimeter-weighted, overweighted, etc. that I use for a full swing shot, but when I need some finesse, I use the old Jack Nicklaus club. I have holed out plenty of shots from off the green with that club. There was one occasion where Ron, Ray and I all hit just to the left of the green. On this particular hole, that is not a bad place to be in that the fairway slopes sharply left to right, and the ocean pull is also in that direction (okay… it's a par 3 and we should be on the green, but we're old guys playing golf). We were lined up neatly in a row, all about 30 feet from the green. I pulled out my trusty Golden Bear PW. Ron had a 7 iron for a pitch-and-run shot, and Ray had his Odyssey putter. I hit a nice chip, but I put a little too much backspin on it and came up shorter than I wanted. Ron, doing what a pro would do (allowing that a pro would find him/her self in this situation in the first place) got the pitch but not the run and also came up short.

Ray got some air with his putter! His ball bounced onto the green and stopped within a gimme distance of the hole for a par!

Ray would rather shoot himself than have to use his PW to get over some obstacle, like a sand trap. He does what I call "triangulation" to get around the obstacle using his putter. When he absolutely has to use his wedge, you can see him shaking as he does his practice swings. He knows he is going to dub it, and he often does (having no confidence is not a good thing in golf, and old guys learn to compensate in all sorts of weird ways).

Gary is quite good with his PW. His only problem is when there is something in the way of his backswing. If he can't wrap both arms around his neck he has trouble.

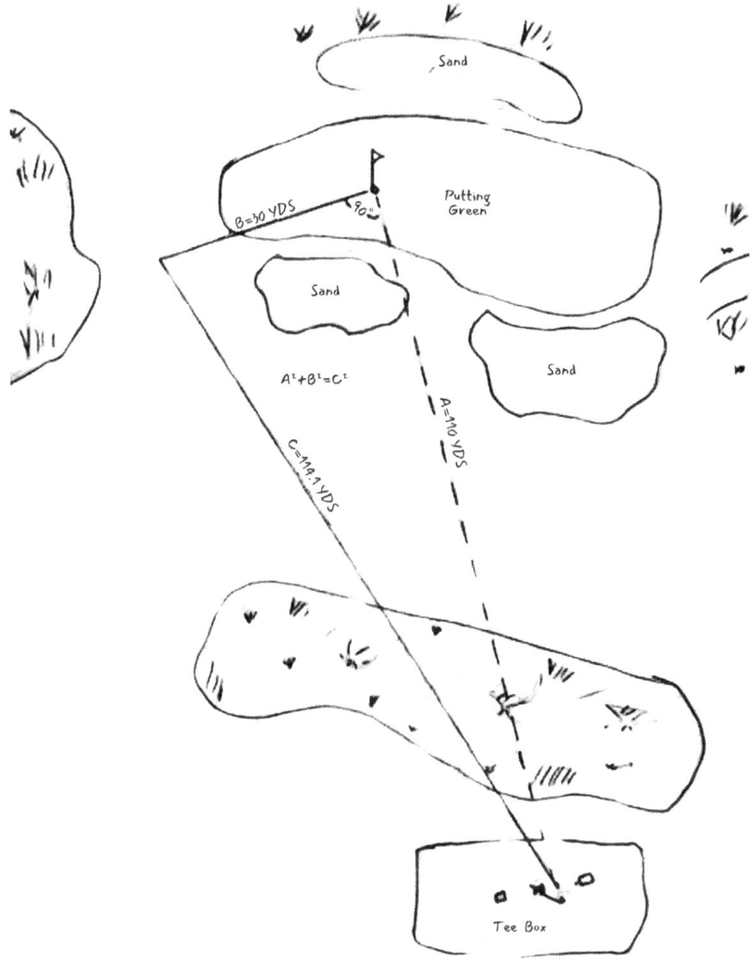

Triangulation Theory

I used to have this wonderful job at Northern Virginia Community College where I taught mostly night classes, and had the daytime to do stuff like playing golf. Of course, I prepared for my classes and did my office duties, but…When the weather was agreeable, I would play three times a week, and I could shoot mid-80s on a regulation course. Then I got a real job (more remunerative, but less free time), and three times a week turned into once a month, then once a year, and my game deteriorated somewhat (it is NOT like riding a bicycle!). Did I mention that I had rotator cuff surgery on my left shoulder a couple of years ago? Anyway, when I retired last year, I had a lot of excuses for not playing well.

Excuses

A professional (at anything) works very hard to identify his or her excuses for losing (or not performing at an optimal level) and then systematically eliminates them. This is the essence of being a professional, and you need to be ruthlessly analytical to do it. I was a professional motorcycle racer for a while, and we had a saying: "If you start the race with an excuse for losing, you will lose."

In golf we tend to focus on the fine details of your grip, your stance and your swing. These can be observed by a good coach and analyzed for continuous improvement. When the solution doesn't feel comfortable, you repeat it endlessly until it becomes second nature. But professionals also work on things like attitude and focus…. less observable, but equally as important. And there are mental exercises that can help. Jack Nicklaus was once asked how he managed to stay so focused for four hours (or more) during a round of golf. His answer was that he can't. But that he can get really focused for about 30 seconds at a time for each swing. When he stepped up to the ball, he knew exactly the shot he was trying to execute, and he had the focus and discipline to execute it perfectly. That is one of the key skills that differentiates a professional golfer from a skilled amateur, or ordinary hackers and mere mortals!

Speaking of mere mortals, that would include us old guys playing golf! We nurture our excuses for playing badly as though they were Congressional Medals of Honor! That way, when a good day and some luck come together to produce a good round, it isn't just a matter of doing what we ought to be doing anyway. It is adversity overcome! It is bravery and courage in the face of obstacles that professionals never encounter. It is the indominable human spirit rising to the challenge of seemingly impossible goals!!!

So, our main excuse is just being old farts! Sadly (only sad in the excuse context!), I'm the least old of the old guys, so I don't get cut much slack in that regard. And my rotator cuff surgery was a few years ago, and it actually healed quite nicely (thank you doctor and Physical Therapy!). But I still have my gimpy left leg (remember the motorcycle racing thing?) to fall back on (sometimes literally). Some days there is the issue of how much wine I drank the night before. When all else fails, I blame the golf ball. But I keep playing it…. if I changed balls and still played like shit that would disprove the bad golf ball theory…. can't let that happen…. my excuse would be gone!

Ray is the oldest of us, and also the shortest, so he has a lot of excuses for not hitting as far as the rest of us. But he is focused. And he often starts a round with a mantra: "No putts left short" … "No sand traps" …. "No 3-putt greens" … "No 6's (our maximum score)." This inevitably results in a reverse psychology situation where he has jinxed everyone! At the end of the round, it serves as an excuse for all of us.

So, for us old farts, our excuses are important and something to be nurtured!

Practice Greens

During COVID the practice greens were closed. This drove me absolutely crazy. I am always certain that my first putt is going to be completely wrong distance-wise. The fact that I am certain makes it a self-fulfilling prophecy and so it happens.

Thankfully the practice greens have reopened, and I park by one that is a little farther from the clubhouse, but chipping practice is allowed there as well. OK, scratch golfers who hit directly from tee-to-green every hole don't really need to worry about this skill, but it comes into play quite often for me, and having confidence in my pitching wedge makes a huge difference in my game. So, I get to the course earlier than everyone else (I live 5 minutes away) and spend a fair amount of time getting my chipping and putting strokes calibrated.

This calibration process is, of course, based on the assumption that the practice green will play the same as the greens on the golf course. And you know what "Assume" means "ASS of U and ME."

Nonetheless, a good golfer wants to warm up and fine tune his/her stroke so the ball contact is square and consistent and the ball at least does what you intended for it to do. It's one thing to misread the green, or choose a landing point for your chip that is not quite right. It is another thing to execute the shot to accomplish what you intended.

Theoretically, success in practice correlates to success on the golf course!

Which brings up the "Old Guys Playing Golf" philosophy of the practice green…. somewhat different. We know that our daily repertoire includes some very good shots and some very bad shots. Our hope is to use up as many of the bad ones as possible on the practice green, so only good ones are left when we head out to the first tee. Personally, if I am doing really well on the practice green…sinking long putts and nearly sinking long chip shots…it worries me! I am using up my daily allotment of good golf shots that I would much rather expend on the actual round. For us old guys, there is sort of golf checking account and when you hit a good shot, that is a withdrawal. I guess professionals have an account as well. Theirs is just better funded than ours!

Scoring

We don't take mulligans, and we're pretty strict about scoring. Ray keeps score, and while he generally asks what we shot after each hole, you can see that he was keeping track in his head. If you happened to forget a penalty stroke or a muffed shot, he will remember it for you. On days when Ray isn't there, or if he has to leave early, then Gary takes over. We figure that an engineer should at least be able to count and add things up correctly! Anything better than bogey golf is considered to be a very good round, but a round under 40 is not bad at all. Over 40 is considered to be a bad round, 40- even is "kissing your sister." However, a round with a birdie in it makes up for everything else! Even with COVID around, a birdie calls for fist bumps all around.

We once shot 27, but that was playing best ball. If you ask Ray what he shot on any given hole, he will respond "Two!" And then add that that got him onto the green, with three putts after that...

I recently had an Eagle!! Which on a Par 3 course means a magical Hole-in-one. After about 40 years of playing golf! Ray gave me the scorecard afterwards, and I realized that my score for the round was 39, with the Ace barely saving me from the embarrassment of being on the wrong side of 40.

Whoever hits the best round gets the scorecard at the end. Sometimes it goes directly into the trash can. But I have a bulletin board at home, and if it actually was a good round, the scorecard goes on it until it is superseded by a better round.... which could take a long time!

On the other hand, if you had high score (that sounds like a good thing.... you have to remember that this is golf!) you are awarded the PINK BALL! That means you must tee off with the pink ball on the first hole of the next round, to the amusement of all of us and any others behind us waiting to tee off. We accept this honor graciously. The best response is to then shoot a "Pink Ball Par[5]" on hole #1 which completely absolves you of any further shame. At that point, the pink ball is retired until the end of the round, at which point it is awarded to its new winner!

Professionals keep track of their score relative to par. You count the variations. So, if, on the front nine, you had one bogey and two birdies, then you are one under par. No need to count all those boring par holes. We, however, are not

---

[5]   After the famous movie, the pink ball has been nicknamed Barbie. We hope for a "Barbie-Birdie."

so blasé about shooting par, and while a par may not be an occasion for fist bumps all around, it is certainly considered to be an accomplishment! I keep track in my head relative to bogey golf. If I hit 5 on 1, 3 and 4, but had two pars, and the rest 4s, then I am at 37, because 36 is "Old guy par" and one real par (3) compensates for one 5!

Ray has a saying: "Four ain't bad." A 4-average would give you a score of 36, which is actually a damn good effort on this course for anyone who is less than professional caliber. And it is certainly well under the 40 threshold of embarrassment!

"Four ain't bad" has its corollaries: "Stinko Cinco" and "Six Sucks." And even the "Four ain't bad" mantra can be downgraded if it followed a brilliant tee shot onto the green, near the pin…and then a 3-putt! Sometimes four sucks…

Distance

Somewhere along the line my clubs stopped hitting the ball as far. I used to be able to count on my 7-iron for 150 yards. Now it's more like 125. I always noticed that old guys hit longer clubs, but I never thought it would happen to me. I now have newer, more modern clubs. Shouldn't they hit the ball farther? They always say that a smooth swing and good ball contact will give you distance, but they forgot to tell my clubs! Maybe the length of a yard has gotten longer? Or maybe they switched to meters but didn't tell anyone…

Of course, some of the fairways are uphill, and sometimes you are hitting into the wind, or the air is damp, which generally means the grass is damp as well, meaning you will get less roll. All important considerations in selecting just the right club. Often after much deliberation and discussing pros and cons with my buddies, I select what I believe is the perfect club, then proceed to dub it into the barranca! I may as well have used my putter!

When the wind is behind us, I will shorten my back-swing and play it more like a finesse chip shot. That is when I really nail the contact and the ball goes off the back of the green and into the sand trap on the other side! Dang!

Carts

We walk the course. Motorized golf carts are not allowed, but they will rent you a push cart for $5.00. Most regular players figure out the math and buy their own carts. Gary and Ray have the expensive 4-wheel drive models that have everything you could want including a cradle for your cell phone and anti-lock brakes. Ron has a 3-wheeled model that still has a lot of new features. Ray loaned me his old cart that has only two wheels (hey, I'm an old motorcycle guy anyway) that looks a little funky but works just fine. It weighs about half what their fancy carts do and goes places where their carts won't fit. Of course, there's no cell phone cradle (hadn't been invented yet) and there's no brakes at all. And the tires would definitely not pass a safety inspection with a tread depth gauge. When it's downhill to the next tee, Gary likes to give his 4WD cart a push and let gravity take it there. Unfortunately, autonomous driving has not been fully integrated into his cart, and it occasionally deviates from his intended path, going into the weeds, or getting up on two wheels like a Joey Chitwood stunt driver.

A few proverbs:

- Luck beats skill
- Straight beats long
- 4 ain't bad (it's a par 3 course)
- A good tee shot is one that is past the ladies[6] tee, and you can find it (sometimes we just settle for being able to find it)
- The golf gods giveth and the golf gods taketh away
- The golf gods punish pride swiftly
- The first shall be last and the last shall be first (regarding honors)
- A lost ball was a no-good ball anyway
- If you are looking for a white ball, and you find a red one, it is yours. It is red from embarrassment.
- You can't expect to hit a long drive from a pink tee
- Intercourse or golf course (Ray, referring to his marital relationship on golf mornings)
- There's no place on the scorecard for style points.

  – A dub that rolls onto the green beats a long, beautiful arcing shot that hits the green and rolls off the back into the sand trap.

---

[6] Making allowances for modern norms, this is assuming that you are hitting from the white or black tees, whether or not you are a lady (woman?). I don't know what the rules are for LGBPQ tees, but in the context of not wanting to offend anyone for any reason, even if the person I'm offending is being offended on behalf of some theoretical other person, let's just say the "Red Tees." (The primary color… No offense to Native Americans intended)

We take turns paying for the round, and I always allow myself 4 strokes off my score if I paid that day. Seems reasonable…there are four of us. That's just 1 stroke p/p.

Some days are cold and rainy. Yes, it's Southern California where it is never supposed to rain, but when you are right next to the ocean, the air can be moist and the wind can be windy. When it is windy, it always seems the be in your face. When you start heading back toward the clubhouse, the wind magically changes direction and is still in your face! Throw in a little light mist, and you have full Southern California golf ambiance. Being "Old guys playing Golf," we make certain allowances for these conditions, knowing that our joints, backbones, wrists, ankles and general body parts don't work as well under these circumstances. We are a little more generous with free drops and "gimme" putts. Into the wind, Ray's low trajectory driver shots begin to make perfect sense, scrupulously avoiding the deleterious effects of the wind at higher altitudes. I find these conditions to be perfect for the "worm-burner" dub that rolls and rolls (lots of top-spin) and completely avoids any aerodynamic influences.

For some reason we like baseball allusions, so whoever has "reverse honors" (last) is "batting clean-up." Various "less-than-perfect" tee shots are described as:

- A pop-fly to the pitcher (or worse still, to the catcher)
- A line drive to the shortstop
- A foul ball to the right grandstand
- A grounder to 2nd base
- A grounder between the pitcher's legs
- A bunt

- A "swing-and-a-miss" - this is embarrassing, but what is even worse is when the wind from the club blows the ball off of the tee. Now you are hitting your 2nd shot, but you can't even use the tee!

Our COVID19 rules allowed us free drops out of the sand traps, but to qualify, your ball had to be resting on the sand. If it was collected by the bear grass surrounding the trap, then you had to "Play it where it lies." This often involved standing on a very steep and uneven slope where simply standing upright was a challenge, let alone swinging a golf club.… let alone actually hitting the ball.… let alone having the ball go anywhere that would be helpful to getting it into the hole. A whiff is always embarrassing, but a whiff that involves losing your balance and falling over into a sand trap is much more embarrassing!

The Provisional

Ray likes the concept of the "Provisional" tee shot. As a younger man, I always thought the term was a euphemism for a Mulligan. But Ray takes it as a serious strategy for dealing with an errant tee shot. Whenever he hits a shot that is A. Out of bounds, or B. Potentially Unfindable, he will hit a provisional shot. And it works for him. Often his Provisional is an excellent shot. He explains: "I'd rather be lying 3 on the green than taking a drop at 3 in the barranca."

Makes sense, except that my "Provisionals" are usually even worse than the shot that caused me to need to take one (whatever was wrong with my swing is still wrong) and now I've lost 2 balls instead of one.

I once played a round with Daryl, my teacher, who encouraged the "Provisional" strategy, even when I was on my 4th attempt! He was supplying the balls, so I was OK with it. After my 4th "Provisional" was shanked into the barranca he admitted that perhaps it was time to move on. After all, there is no reason to practice bad shots!

"I think I can find it"

I am known as "I think I can find it." Ray says he will engrave that on my headstone when I am dead! That's what I say when I hit a ball into the weeds. With the help of my friends, I often CAN find it, and sometimes the lie is playable. Some of my best shots have been from stupid lies in the middle of deep undergrowth and weeds. I use my sand wedge to blast through the weeds and often find myself on the green with a makeable par putt. This is where extra notations on the score card really should be recorded, like the box score for a baseball game. I tell Ray to put a "U" (for UGLY) next to my actual score.

HOLE	1	2	3	4	5	6	7	8	9	Tot	Hcp	Net
BACK	123	104	172	136	115	145	150	173	121	1239		
MIDDLE	93	84	145	118	97	127	111	157	105	1037		
HANDICAP	9	6	1	3	5	8	4	2	7			
GARY	4	6	6	4	4	6	6	4	5	45		
TOM	2	3	4	6	4	3	4	4	4	34		
RON	6	4	4	5	5	4	4	6	5	43		
RAY	3	3	4	4	5	3	4	4	6	36		
PAR	3	3	3	3	3	3	3	3	3	27		
FORWARD	65	63	86	87	74	90	83	106	62	716		
HANDICAP	9	6	1	3	5	8	4	2	7			
FOOT GOLF	73	88	64	79	89	65	57	115	65	695		

L = LUCKY
U = UGLY

SCORER: _______________

ATTEST: _______________ DATE: 3/21   Ⓢ SHOT SELECTOR

When I find myself in "I think I can find it" mode, Ray's first question is "what kind of ball are we looking for?" I've learned to reply "One that is in a playable lie." I've found that the Titleist that I hit off the tee sometimes morphs into a Taylor Made while interacting with the fauna and flora, and that this is a natural phenomenon of golf courses that is associated with the lunar cycle of internal golf ball rotation. It is no different than the changing of the seasons, plants flowering and going to seed, rabbits mating…all part of nature's plan.

At the end of a round, we either celebrate or commiserate and try to find reasons to not give up golf altogether and take up bowling. I take some pride in managing to play the whole round with the same ball. If we got through the round with no scores of 6, that is something to celebrate. Then there is the golf ball "lost-to-found" ratio. Sometimes the absence of any sports injuries is the best we can do…

Golf Balls

Ray buys everything from Costco so we know that the Kirkland ball must be his. I showed off my new golf glove one morning and Ray, being Ray, asked me how much I paid for it. I knew what was coming! I responded honestly that I paid about $20 at the clubhouse and he chided me that I could have bought 4 of them at Costco for that price! I didn't know that, but the next time my wife and I were at Costco I checked it out…. it's true!

People like to personalize their golf balls in interesting ways. There are a zillion different logo balls, with USC Trojan logos, IBM, Fidelity Investments, etc. I found one that had the NFL Players Association on it! But the most interesting things are what people add with magic markers. Lots of "smiley faces," initials and that sort of thing, but there are also various images that seem to be hoping for divine (the sign of the cross) or demonic (voodoo) intervention! Then there was the ball with a voluptuous pair of tits drawn on it, apparently to help the golfer (presumably male) keep his attention on the ball during his backswing. There are dots, squiggles and other personalization, intended to make sure that his Titleist 77 TOUR doesn't get confused with anyone else's…all for naught since I found it in the barranca!

I found one ball that had "Biden[7] Sucks" written on it with magic marker. It was the first time I had seen a golf ball used as a vehicle of political commentary, and it made me wonder about the political demographics of golfers, and what percentage would agree or disagree with the author's eloquent assessment of our current president. My gut feeling is that golf is more of a republican sport, but I have no proof of that. But if it is true, it might present an untapped marketing opportunity for political advertisers!

How do I know all of this? Because we find a lot of lost balls while searching for our own. Sometimes we find "nests" where the balls appear to have multiplied on their own. There is a certain joy in finding more balls than you lost during a round (though I prefer the joy of having played the entire round with the same ball). However, I refer to these "found" balls as "feral," because we have rescued them from the wild, and you have to understand that they are fundamentally undomesticated and they will eventually succumb to their feral nature and return to the wild. A feral ball will take unexpected hooks, slices or bad bounces to seek out the wil-

---

[7]   Interestingly, Trump National Golf Course is only a couple of miles down the road. Perhaps the ball was purchased there?

derness areas of the golf course. They are looking for a mate. Or perhaps they just tire of being hit…

Hole 8 at Bella Mare goes past the school range, and some range balls find their way onto the fairway, or even the green. There is a moral quandary that can occur when you think your ball is lying pretty, and pick it up and find a range ball, leaving you to wonder where your real ball actually ended up….

Speaking of that hole, it has a wonderful feature that we call the "automatic ball return." If you hit left, and just a little long, there is a swale. If you find yourself at the bottom of the swale, chip up on to the green, but just a little short, it will roll back down to your feet and you will not even need to move for your next shot. It is deceiving because the green looks as though it slopes to the right, but "ocean suck" pulls it left and brings it right back to you! If you were there to practice your chip shots, it would save you a lot of walking. If, on the other hand, you were hoping to get a decent score, it is quite frustrating!

Moral Quandaries

Golf is full of moral quandaries. The scorecard is unforgiving and leaves no place for style points, great recoveries, or 1/2-strokes. We have all had a birdie putt go partly into the hole, run around the rim and then pop out a half-inch away. I think that should count as 0.5 strokes! Of course, the rules make no provision for fractional strokes… Then there is your lie. If you hit a good tee shot that may not be on the green, but is close enough to putt, you shouldn't have to worry about the sprinkler head that is on your putting line, should you?

I worried about that duck…the Mo#$% Fuc#@! screwed up my shot and I thought a little bit of pain would serve him right, but I didn't actually want to injure him, at least not after I got over being pissed off…

I know that a drop is supposed to have a random outcome, and there are strict rules about how it should be executed so an unfair advantage is not gained from it. But hey…. we do this for fun, right? I might occasionally influence my drop to find a more playable lie.

I was brought up Catholic, so I understand guilt quite well. The nuns knew how to make little boys feel guilty about almost everything having to do with being little boys! Then there was confession. What can a 6-year-old kid really have to confess? I remember telling the priest that I had committed a sin against the 6th commandment (Thou shalt not commit adultery!) because I couldn't think of anything to confess and you are supposed to confess something. I had no idea what adultery was, but I knew it was naughty so I must have transgressed it at some point. The priest laughed. He told me to say 5 Hail Marys and to think of something better next time!

Golf courses should have confessionals at the club house. And they should sell indulgences! It might be good business!

Your Lie

The term sounds like your dishonesty, but in golf it can present incredible technical (or moral) quandaries when a really good shot arcs gracefully into the air, lands just off the green (as you intended, so it will roll onto the green) and gets stuck in some mud (thwack) leaving you with a downhill line to the green and an impossible club-contact scenario.

The fairways at Bella Mare are very well maintained and present beautiful swathes of well-mowed green grass (except during the aforementioned aeration periods). Should you happen to misjudge the distance to the green and land a little short, or (more likely) dub your tee shot and have it roll out into the fairway, hopefully past the Ladies' Tee, you find yourself playing off this verdant expanse of soft, springy grass…perfect for a chip shot onto the green, and maybe right into the hole for a birdie! However, as you walk up to your ball, you become aware of minor imperfections in the grassy surface, and inevitably, thanks to the forces of gravity, inertia and the malevolence of the golf gods, your ball has found one of them and is sitting on the only bit of hard dirt that you can see, with the lovely grass on all sides of it…now blocking your swing! This presents another moral quandary…if I just happened to nudge the ball out of the hole it is in and up onto the beautiful grass surface, that would surely be what the course designers intended to happen, wouldn't it?

Then there are the places the ball manages to find in the barranca. Sometimes it is hopelessly buried in a bush…no question of trying to hit it without taking a drop. But other times I think "It's crazy, but it just might work!" The sand wedge can do amazing things if it can get under the ball…. the rocks…. the large plants…. over the large plants…these shots are not for the faint of heart. You need to strike the ball firmly and decisively…a little Hail Mary ahead of time doesn't hurt, but don't just close your eyes! I've learned that, in the course of addressing the ball, you might need to stand on some of the obstructive plants…not actually removing them or ripping them out, or attacking them with a machete (the natural temptation, which would violate the rules) but merely finding footing for your swing that just happens to open up a line for your ball to travel…assuming that you actually hit the ball…

At some point Gary, a great friend and the best man at my wedding, nonetheless decided that we needed to treat the left of the cart path as "Out of Bounds" with dire penalties (2 strokes) for landing there! We play all the other holes with environmental signs saying we should avoid these areas (as though we hit there on purpose) and there are always ground under repair signs, etc. But this particular situation seems to invoke an inviolable rule for Gary. And while he rarely questions Ray's (The DA) authority on such matters, we all respect his opinion in this matter. I have learned to shank right rather than hook to avoid the horrible shame of being OB. Personally, if I were playing by myself…. I would discreetly chip off the OB dirt…onto the green… maybe into the hole??? I would count that as a birdie in my mental scorecard.

Sometimes your ball is sitting in the open (you can find it!) but the lie is backed up to some obstruction (bushes, tall grass, cactus, etc.) so that it has a good potential flight path in front of it, but not much possibility of a backswing. This drives Gary crazy and he will almost certainly take a drop and the corresponding stroke rather than attempt the shot. I criticize Gary because he is far more used to hitting the ball onto or near the green and thus has little or no practice at this technique. I, on the other hand, somehow manage to find myself in this situation more frequently, and thus, have more experience at dealing with the circumstances. You need to sneak your club (usually a sand wedge) between the obstruction and the ball, maybe push the club down into the dirt a little, then swing from that point, contacting the ball, and doing a huge follow through, as though the club was a shovel and you were picking the ball up and flinging it into the air. This shot is never going to get on the green from 100 yards out, but it has gotten me onto the green from 20 yards!

Sometimes I ask myself why I am so good at shots from difficult lies??? Practice, practice, practice…

When my tee shot has me near, but not actually on, the green, my default is to use my pitching wedge…my beloved Jack Niklaus Golden Bear pitching wedge. I have a much newer wedge that is perimeter-weighted, counter-weighted and over-weighted. I use it for a full swing shot. But for a finesse shot I have confidence in the old wedge and I usually manage to do a little warm-up with it before starting the round, at a practice green that allows chipping. However, sometimes the lie can be deceptive, with a thin layer of limp, flaccid grass covering hard adobe mud. Often the grass is mashed flat against the mud, giving you no space at all to get your club underneath the ball without digging into the HARD mud. This takes away all of your finesse and almost guarantees that you will dub the ball, hit it all the way across the green, and into the sand trap or drainage ditch or some other horrible fate on the other side. Given the same proximity to the green, Ray always hits his putter, and I have learned that sometimes it is the right thing to do. Maybe wisdom does come with age. But I'm not sure wisdom is quite the right word. It's more like getting tired of fighting the reality of your skill set all the time.

One of my lessons from Daryl is that a muffed putt is never as bad as a muffed chip.

OK.…it's a Par 3 course and theoretically you shouldn't have to worry about your lie because you are supposed to hit it onto the green from the tee. Maybe that would just be boring? I'll never know.

The Tee Boxes

The course does an excellent job of maintaining the grass, but it can be a challenge in the tee area, because it is natural to take a divot when teeing off, and not everyone is as meticulous as I am about replacing their divots! This means that today's tee box will be pretty chewed up tomorrow, so it needs to move around to give the grass a chance to grow back. This is perfectly understandable and should be respected as good golf course maintenance.

HOWEVER… mornings when it appears that the guy doing the pin locations had reason to be grumpy (didn't get any?) seem to coincide with tee box locations that just happen to give you the worst possible angle at the green and pin location. e.g. #5 (scene of my Hole-in-one!) has two bunkers on the right side of the green, and the pin is sometimes located behind them. Daryl would hit his sand wedge over the traps, land it on the green next the hole, and have enough backspin on the ball to make it stop there. No problem!

I know from experience, however, that if you come in from the left side of the green, the ball will run to the right (the ocean sucks!) and get you right up to that pin without needing the cojones to hit up and over those all-devouring sand traps!

Oh, but the same grumpy guy put the tee box markers all the way on the right, so you pretty much have to hit over the sand traps. There is a tiny peninsula between them which I have managed to land the ball on and have it roll onto the green with its speed having been reduced by the longer grass…. this is a "Fortune favors the brave"[8] shot and there are a lot of ways for it to go wrong!!!

"Fortune favors the brave"

At some point I began a Bolshevik Revolution and decided to ignore the arbitrary and capricious nature of the tee box location, noticing virginal, grassy areas way to the left where my angle on the green would actually make sense with how the green plays, avoiding the cavernous sand traps rather than inviting disaster.

---

[8] "Fortune favors the brave" (attributed to Julius Caesar) was the tagline for a Superbowl commercial about virtual currency and trading agencies. NFTs (Non-Fungible Tokens) have since had great difficulties with billions of dollars lost and various people going to jail… and I have learned to remind my golf ball that it is "fungible!"

Gary frowned at this behavior, but realized its merit. Rather than defy the rules, he uprooted the tee box markers and moved them so my improvised tee-off area became official!

Course Personnel

It's good to get to know the course personnel, and Ray always calls and gets our situation of who is teeing off ahead of us and how we will know that we are up next. We take turns buying the round, rather than have each of us having to check in individually. It makes a lot of sense actually, and saves us and the golf course a lot of trouble. It is possible to pay online, and that's what the other guys do. I do not. Why not? You might ask. Noelle! Very cute and pretty, friendly and nice as can be, has taken over morning desk duties, and I may be old, but I'm not dead yet…so I pay in person! Doing business online has a lot of advantages, but there are still good, practical reasons for face-to-face transactions. BTW - she wore a mask when it was required during COVID restrictions. She had big brown eyes that managed to smile (without actually seeing the rest of her face) and make you feel as though she might have enjoyed the conversation. Eventually the mask requirement went away… first for us clients, then, finally for the course personnel. I remember checking in and saying: "Noelle! You have a face!" She smiled radiantly and seemed to be happy that I had noticed…I had a good round that day!

Jessica drives the big-rig course mowing machine. She knows our names and says hi, and if she is mowing the fairway ahead of us when we are teeing off, she pulls discreetly to the side and waves us through. She even applauds when one of us manages a good shot. For me there is something about knowing that a girl is watching and not wanting to look stupid that seems to help with my focus. I often hit good shots when Jessica is watching! Sadly, her male counterparts don't have the same effect. In fact, they seem to not even notice that we are waiting on them to tee off. When this is the case, I wait for them to be blocking the sand trap in front of the green before I hit my tee shot!

There is a Falconer at Bella Mare! Kind of an old hippie guy who drives a Bella Mare golf cart with hotel guests around the golf course with his bird and a 3-legged dog. He is often at the 7th tee with his clients, having released his bird into the air. He gets out of our way to let us tee off, but it is fascinating to watch him work with his falcon. He has a feathered dummy on a rope that he swings around and throws into the air, which gets the bird to swoop down on it…. sort of like throwing a stick for a dog, but in three dimensions. He has this thick leather glove on one hand where the bird sits when it is not flying around. I see him and wonder about this arcane skill, how he learned it, and the fact that he appears to be making a living with it! He makes about $150/hr pp! I wonder how much of that the bird gets??

We have had various guys (and one woman) working as starters. We are out early enough and out on the practice green so we don't interact much at the beginning of the round. But at the end he or she is always waiting. The really nice ones come over and clean up our golf clubs for us. And there is always the question: "So, how was your round?" Various responses:

- "Flashes of brilliance, interrupted by comic relief." (Translation: "I made at least one good shot, probably compensating for a bad tee shot.")
- "The weather was great." (Translation: "I played like shit.")
- "Ray had a good round" (Translation: "I did not.")

- "The birdies were in the trees, but not on the score card." (Translation: "I missed 4 birdie putts.")
- "Birdied #9!" (Translation: "I played like shit until then, but now I have a reason to come back!")
- "Played the whole round with the same ball!" (Translation: "And that is all I have to feel good about.")
- "Stupid game!" (No translation needed!)
- "What a beautiful day!" (Translation: "We all played like shit.")
- "I paid for the round. That gives me three strokes off my score, right?" (Translation: "I shot 42, 39 is our minimum expectation."
- "The greens are really fast today." (Translation: "I putted badly.")
- "The greens are really slow today." (Same as above)

Aerating the course

Golf courses need maintenance. This is an undeniable fact… and it gives us more excuses[9] for dealing with conditions that require compensatory rules (sic Ray). This April, they reduced our green fees because the greens had been aerated (that means they have been run over with a machine that puts 3/8" holes, 1" apart, all over the green, then covered in sand, for the purpose of promoting the growth of the peculiar and unique variety of grass that is used for golf greens) which means that the predictability of your putt distance and direction has a whole new level of randomness! Ray (the district attorney) pronounced that there will be no 3-putts under these condi-

---

[9]   See section on Excuses

tions. Ray (the Putt Meister) then proceeded to start sinking 30' putts and shot his best round ever for the course!

The discount stopped…. Ray considered this to be the factor that determined the 2- putt rule…but the course aeration did not. Now it was the fairways, with giant dirt/hard clay turds all over the grass between you and the green. OK…I know it is a par 3 course and you are supposed to just hit the ball into the air and land it on the green with enough backspin to make it stay right next to the pin for a gimme birdie…Then there is real life for "Old Guys Playing Golf" where a lucky dub and a bowling shot sometimes plays out well, with no place on the scorecard to indicate the lack of style points! The dirt clods pretty much kill the bowling strategy, and they also interfere with Ray's "putt from 30 feet off the green" strategy. We haven't yet figured out a compensatory rule for this situation…

Pin Placement

When you play the same course all the time, you might think that there are no variables, and you can home in on perfection! There should be some truth to that and I like to think that I know the idiosyncrasies of Bella Mare better than most. However, there are seasonal and "course maintenance" issues, but the most notable and obvious difference on a day-to-day basis is the pin placement.

There are sand traps…I think I mentioned this earlier but I will say it again…some of them are downright mean! BUT if you place the pin with a sand trap directly between you and the tee-box…well that is just cruel! Some mornings we think to ourselves that whoever was placing these holes did not get laid this morning and was clearly feeling grumpy!

Daryl told me that the key to Par 3 golf was height and backspin. Hit the ball way up in the air, land it very near the pin, and have enough backspin to stop it there, rather than rolling off the back of the green and into the sand trap. If you can master this approach, the sand trap in between is irrelevant.

Fine…. some days I'm feeling confident and go for it. As often as not, my gracefully arcing shot lands a foot short of my target and rolls into the front sand trap…. or I get it a little "thin" and it lands on the green, but rolls off the back…. into another sand trap. Then I look at Ray's "triangulation" approach and wonder if that isn't a better idea…

Fauna

There are always birdies in the trees, if not on the scorecard. These include red winged blackbirds and finches that are lovely songbirds. Then there are sandpipers that hop around the tee boxes and greens in a way that is very cute. There are a fair number of hawks, including a domesticated one that works with a falconer who entertains hotel guests. We once saw an eagle surveying the 8th fairway! Looking out over the water, we see squadrons of pelicans, cruising about an inch above the water searching for their breakfast.

Crows are not "birdies!" Yes, they are of the ornithological persuasion, but they are not "birdies." Nothing cute about them. They like to gather around while we are teeing off, and they caw in a way that sounds remarkably like they are laughing at us…

In the spring we get bunnies: cute, furry, long-eared, cotton-tailed bunnies. True to their species' survival strategy, they multiply prolifically and are extremely timid. Of course, there are those hawks, and the resort has a French Restaurant! Lapin le Coucou anyone? Things are also damp in the spring and there are several places where you can hear the chirping sound that frogs make.

The really good golfers who hit from tee-to-green every time miss a lot of this interaction with nature that is so good for the soul!

Interestingly, when we are teeing off, the birds tend to flee to the green, knowing instinctively that it is the safest place for them to avoid being hit by a golf ball!

We sometimes play a course in Manhattan Beach (very high-class place!) that is part of a lovely hotel ambiance and has some water features that come into play on the golf course. That is where I had my interaction with a duck (mentioned earlier) but there are also geese who frequent the 7th fairway, and generally like to cross the fairway as a family as we are teeing off. The family hierarchy is quite clear with Monsieur Goose leading the way, Madame Goose behind and multiple goslings in tow. Ever so cute… but we know that geese adore golf greens, and love to spend their time there, apparently after having digested their meals… their leavings are a problem when trying to putt!

Flora

Golf courses are almost always pleasant places to be, with great expanses of green grass, glorious views of the surrounding countryside and a very park-like ambiance. I remember playing golf at The Greenbrier in West Virginia with the dogwood trees in full bloom. They have these beautiful white blossoms….and I hit my tee shot a little to the right, near one of these beautiful trees…. with their white flower petals all over the grass….and my white golf ball somewhere amongst them…eventually the beauty subsumed into the frustration of not being able to find my ball that I knew was right there!!!!

Golf courses in the east also have more wooded areas and corresponding undergrowth than they do in the west. The beauty of these areas, with forsythias and azaleas in the spring and the glorious foliage of the maple and oak trees in the fall cannot be underestimated. It is truly sublime and completely makes up for the humidity and the mosquitos that go along with this ambiance (fall is best!).

Then there is the poison ivy. It is a very clever plant that grows along the edge of wooded areas where a less-than-perfect tee shot might land, knowing that it's victims will A. Not recognize it from among the other semi-shade plants. B. Cover just enough of the ball that you can see it, but you will reach in and pick it up to take a drop, rather than try to hit it from its lie. The unsuspecting tourist now has a 2-week, nasty, itchy, case of poison ivy that will ooze and be miserable! I was a Boy Scout in the east and I recognize it. I learned that you use a wedge to get the ball out of the poison ivy, then you don't touch the blade of that wedge until you have found a water hazard in which to wash it off! (BTW - golf courses in the east always have lots of water hazards…great breeding grounds for birds, frogs and mosquitos).

I believe that nature, and natural things are good…but Mother Nature has her bitchy side and she must have been pissed off at human beings when she came up with poison ivy! (and mosquitos).

Thankfully we don't have that in California (for the taxes we pay we should have everything be perfect every day!!!) But we have our own coastal beauty (never mind the backed-up container ships in the channel) with cactus, bougainvillea, jacaranda, oleander, various daisies and un-named flowering bushes. The ambiance is very different from eastern courses, but the broad expanses of green grass remain, and the ocean views are quite nice, apart from how the pull screws up our putts!

These plants all have their defense mechanisms, bearing out my theory about Mère Nature. The long grasses have very sharp edges and the flowering bushes have thorns that will draw blood. If you have a bad day with multiple barranca shots, you could wind up needing a blood transfusion…

Professional Golf

Ordinary Joes like us fantasize about being professionals, even though we are old farts. We might be old, but we're not dead yet! But my analogies tend to be from Jack Nicklaus rather than Rory McIlroy…what would Jack do in this situation? Or calling for the ball to do the famous Fuzzy Zoeller roll-back down the slope…or Lee Trevino's advice about lining up putts (toward your left foot if it is going to break left-to-right, toward your right foot if is going to break right-to-left)

We talk about whatever PGA Tournament happened over the weekend (haven't yet had a chance to discuss a LIV tournament!) and what do we discuss you might ask? How Rory scored by banking his shot off a wall, how Scheffler missed a 3-foot putt, how Spieth shanked a shot into the crowd….in short, how these professionals sometimes screw up just like us ordinary mortals and how luck sometimes beats skill just as it does for us. There is a great quote from Gary Player about the role of luck in golf: "I'm certain there is an amount of luck in golf, but all I know for sure is that the more I practice the luckier I get." Good advice for more than just golf!

Often, we finish our round and see the staff setting up tables and chairs. We immediately assume that they are for our autograph sessions that will almost certainly follow our round. There must be some adoring fans somewhere…. that's why we do this, right? Helicopters do cover our rounds occasionally. Of course, they are Coast Guard helicopters and not ESPN. Just as well. They always show up after a shot into the barranca. Sometimes they are police helicopters that appear to be searching for escaped convicts on the golf course, which gives us a good feeling….

Anyway, when you play a hole where you hit the ball onto the green and miss your birdie putt by an inch or so, you start thinking that this game isn't so hard and I could do this better than those chumps on TV. Or when you hole out a chip shot from off the green…or when your bunker shot hits the pin and falls into the hole…humility usually follows shortly thereafter. Daryl, my coach, shot a 26 on the round we played together, but failed to qualify for a professional tournament in Palm Springs. The reality of being a professional golfer is pretty damn tough.

No harm in fantasizing though!

Humility

I went to Catholic school and learned that humility was a virtue and that pride was a vice. My subsequent life experiences did little to reinforce these teachings (spike the football in the endzone, etc.) but I think that if humility is truly an important virtue, then all children should be taught to play golf.[10]

We often discuss the "Golf Gods" and their obvious interference in our rounds. We all speak to our shots while they are in flight or rolling on the golf course surface, encouraging the ball to behave like a good dog and stop where it is told. But the Gods are sometimes angry…. particularly if you shot birdie on the previous hole…and the ball can take amazing bounces that lead into cavernous sand traps… or worse.

But humility is important. If you can't deal with humility then you are playing the wrong game! Before I retired, I was told that a bad day of golf is better than a good day at work. I've had some pretty damn good days at work and some pretty awful days at golf, so I'm not sure I can corroborate that. But there are some rounds where I have to remind myself that the ambiance is quite beautiful and the score of my round means little in the grand scheme of life…a humble, Zen-like point of view that doesn't usually last very long with me…

If all children were all taught to play golf there would be a lot of advantageous outcomes:

- They would learn to appreciate and respect open spaces
- They would learn eye-hand coordination skills that are useful
- They would learn the value of using a tool (golf club) to accomplish a goal

______

[10]   My wife was a nun when she was younger. In the nunnery they had a nun-joke about being "proud of their humility!"

- They would learn some degree of patience…to be meticulous about executing a skill
- They would learn valuable life lessons about doing things properly.…and that that doesn't always guarantee the result. (Dang!)

So that's where the humility lesson comes in. I used to teach car salespeople how to sell Honda cars, which were pretty easy to sell because they were pretty good cars and people wanted to buy them. The average close rate was about 20%, but the top salespeople did more like 50%. One of the lessons was that even the top people had to deal with rejection, shake it off, and get on with things. They say that one of the requirements for a professional football quarterback is to have a very short memory… "I just got sacked and slammed to the ground by several 300+ lb. guys, and I now need to try that again.… sure…I can do that!"

I think that patience and humility go together and are important in perfecting a skill. Personally, I never had much of either, so perfection remains elusive. I do get to the golf course on the early side and get in some chipping and putting practice (remember my Gary Player quote).

Golf and Sex

It's inevitable…a game that involves balls, holes, strokes, various lengths of things (club shafts, etc.), and satisfaction, or lack thereof, and put four old guys together who at least remember about sex, and the allusions are going to happen.

Allowing for the fact that we are four old GUYS playing golf, the subject of one's putter, and how good you are with it tends to come up. I believe this can be attributed to Johnny Carson from a Tonight Show episode where he was interviewing a famous golfer's wife. He asked if she did anything special for him before a tournament, and she replied "I kiss his balls." Johnny Carson looked at the camera with one of his unforgettable expressions (I can't just let this go…), then turned to her and asked "Doesn't that make his putter stand up?" So now, having hit onto the green, it is time to "whip out" your putter.

Then there is the wet spot. We play in the morning and they are often running the sprinklers, leaving dampness in the swales and lower areas on the course. If your ball happens to land in one these areas, your hopes for the ball to bounce or roll onto the green are dashed! So, avoiding the wet spot becomes an important part of your tee shot strategy. However, I like to point out that a gentleman would purposely occupy the wet spot in order to spare his partner the discomfort…

"That's what she said." An oft repeated phrase amongst men after finding that your tee is too short, your shot is too short, or almost anything is of a magnitude less than expected. Examples:

- "That was the shortest drive of the week" - that's what she said
- "You peaked too soon" - that's what she said
- "Your putter seems weak today" - that's what she said (also, there are little blue pills you can take for that)

- "That tee must be 6 inches long" - that's what she said (it's really 3 inches!)
- "I need to wash my balls" - that's what she said
- "I can't seem to get it into the hole today" - that's what she said. You get the idea…

A putter length is important for us because it represents the all-important "gimme putt" parameter that can save us from the ignominy of missing a really short putt, and spare us all from watching Ray spend 15 minutes lining up a 2-foot putt. But of course, the length of your putter is supposed to correlate to the length of your fingers…

We occasionally see women golfers ahead of us, or catching us up from behind because we are playing slowly. Once in a while one or more of them is worth scoping out. Gary remarks that he is enjoying looking at her, but he forgets why…

We have an expression for when the wind is blowing in your face that goes "Up your club!" It just means that if you usually hit a 9-iron, you might want to hit an 8 or a 7, but it sounds gratifyingly rude.

But enough of such tawdry discussions and back to the serious subject of playing the noble game from Scotland!

$\Delta p \Delta q \approx \mathbf{h}$

Quantum theory and golf

The Heisenberg Uncertainty Principle refers to quantum physics, not golf, and I'm pretty sure that Werner Heisenberg did not play golf, being far too busy with Einsteinian physics to worry about such mundane amusements as trying to hit a little ball into a slightly bigger hole.

Nonetheless, the concept that the more you know about the physical location of a particle, the less you know about its energy and velocity, and vice versa seems to ring true with golf. If we think of a golf ball as a photon that we are aiming at the green, and ultimately at the flagstick, you would assume that a straight line would be the logical trajectory. Unfortunately, our photons are affected by various influences of both the STRONG FORCE (Gravity) and the *weak force* (should be electromagnetism, but in our case, it is the wind). A skilled golfer (or his caddy) can do his best to calculate acceleration, terminal velocity and direction to predict the p in the equation, that is **Position**. This is, in fact what professionals do, and they practice swing after swing with coach and video feedback to ensure that the forces applied to our golfing equivalent of a photon are precisely what is required to achieve p with a high degree of certainty.

Then there are Old Guys Playing Golf, where Heisenberg's principle comes into play more strongly. There seems to be a much higher degree of uncertainty about the forces applied to the ball, resulting in acceleration, vector, velocity and p (position) that are fairly random. And you would think that simple ballistics would accurately predict the outcome, but that ignores the effect of the STRONG FORCE on our golfing photon, which reacts disproportionately to various BLACK HOLES around the golf course. The most obvious is a sand trap. Any experienced golfer knows that a golf ball that lands in front of the green on a trajectory leading onto the green will, given the choice between bouncing straight onto the green, or bouncing sideways into a sand trap, will almost always take the second choice. A barranca area, or an out-of-bounds area exhibit a similar gravitational pull where the ball's behavior seems to defy its ballistic inertia and validate Mr. Heisenberg's equation.

Many people confuse the Heisenberg Uncertainty Principle with the similar "Observer Phenomenon" which states that the act of observing a quantum event affects its outcome. It simply states that if there is an interaction between quantum particles that has two or more possible outcomes, the act of observing will force one of the outcomes to happen. In other words, purely objective observation is impossible. I used to bring this principle up at work when we discussed the customer satisfaction surveys that were all the rage in business at the time. I think they still are, but they have been reduced to absurdity with thumbs up or down likes/dislikes. We went through lots of permutations of surveys trying to identify true consumer sentiment, with the results (costing millions of dollars!) yielding mostly confusion. I believe the truth is, as in quantum physics, that there is no way to observe and measure human behavior that does not bias the outcome.

So back to golf. You are playing by yourself, and catch up to a foursome, who politely invite you to play through, having noticed that you are playing well. As you tee off, you are aware of the assumption that has been made, so you try to hit a good, clean shot, so you can continue on and not hold up these nice people who have let you play through. Ahhhh, but the Observer Phenomenon comes into play now. The odds of you hitting a good shot become drastically reduced, and the odds of you hitting an embarrassingly bad shot increase dramatically.

On the other hand, there was Jessica, one of the grounds keepers at Bella Mare who drove a mower and would politely pull off to the side when we were teeing off (some of the men drivers would just go on with their mowing and ignore us, inviting us to try to hit them!) I think all four of us guys reacted to being observed by a girl in a positive manner. It is one thing to screw up in front of someone else. It is another thing to screw up in front of a girl (us being guys) who you want to impress! In each case, the quantum "Observer Phenomenon" is borne out in golf quantum theory.

Why do we put ourselves through this torture?

How many sports can really old guys still play? Football, basketball, baseball, soccer, hockey…all meant for guys in their 20's, maybe 30's. 40 is definitely too old! With golf, your skills and strength may deteriorate some with age, but experience and strategy can make up for some of that. There are some really old guys who are still scratch golfers. Not us of course…but we each have a very good round once in a while. So, one reason we do this is because we can! The satisfaction of reaching down to pick up your ball from the hole way exceeds the pain of having to bend over that far!

A man (or a woman) should have a challenge. My buddies and I are all retired and have had plenty of challenges in our lives. You might think we would be happy to settle for getting our underwear on in the morning facing the right direction as our biggest challenge! But I have learned that as you get old, you have to keep reminding your body that you are not done with it yet, because Mother Nature intended for you to be done before 40! If you don't push yourself physically once in a while, your body will quite happily punch its time card and say goodbye!

But golf is also a mental challenge, and that is just as important. Golf is a psycho-motor skill. The motor skill, muscle memory, eye-hand coordination part is important, but without the compensatory adjustments of aim, reading the green, allowing for the wind direction, etc. and decision-making (should I aim for the pin, or hit left of the sand trap?) you still won't be a good golfer. A beautiful, arcing tee shot that goes over the green and into the barranca behind gets style points, but not a good golf score! And just as with your body, you need to keep reminding your brain that you are not done with it yet!

You need a reason to get your butt up out of bed and out of the house! Entropy tends to take over as we move from a youthful, high-energy state to an old-fart, low energy state. Most physicists don't realize this, but the force of gravity increases as you get older, especially later in the day! Things that used to be easy for me to lift have become more difficult, and climbing the stairs requires more strength! What other explanation could there be? This is a facet of the Theory of Relativity that Einstein didn't fully explain, but it is quite clear to me. Anyway, having paid for a round of golf provides the external force that overcomes the inertial force of being a body at rest.

It's good to hang with your buds. You could just as easily hang with your buds in front of the TV and eat pizza and drink beer…maybe bet on the game for a challenge. But having peer pressure to get out and do something is better. I sometimes play golf by myself. There is a certain Zen-like serenity to it…and nobody knows or cares if I improve my lie! But having a really good round by yourself is like kissing your sister. It's nice, but it doesn't mean anything! When you are playing well, you really want your buddies to be around to witness it. Of course, there is the other side of that coin. But they say misery loves company! To win the pink ball is to have surpassed mediocrity and achieved a level where only improvement is possible. The pink ball is an acknowledgement of that achievement from my fellow old guys!

Acknowledgements

First and foremost, I must thank my great friends and golf buddies who provided me with inspiration to write this book and the sometimes-ridiculous content that made it fun. We all met at a wine tasting bar in Torrance, CA called the Liquor Barn, and the friendships we made there have endured for well over 30 years. Gary and his wife stood up for my wife and I and I at our wedding (met her at the same place!). Ray and his wife have hosted the best 4th of July parties in the world for the past 30 years and Ron and his wife Gayle are the most gracious hosts and generous people you could ever hope to meet.

Thank you, guys, for letting me make fun of your (and my) foibles and general love/hate relationship with the game of golf.

As I was drafting the book, it became clear to me that it needed some illustrations. My artistic talent doesn't go far beyond stick-men. I can draw anything that only needs a ruler, so I can do a pretty good sketch of a Tesla Cyber Truck. Beyond that I am hopeless. I realized I needed help from a professional. That turned out to be more difficult than I thought. After several frustrating tries and a lot of time wasted, I came across Polestar Designs. Manhoor A. did most of the illustrations, with us communicating electronically, me in California and her in Pakistan! Thank you Manhoor!

Finally, I would like to thank the staff at The Links at Bella Mare Resort in Rancho Palos Verdes, CA for running a beautiful golf course and treating us like honored guests no matter how badly we play.

www.ingramcontent.com/pod-product-compliance
Lightning Source LLC
Chambersburg PA
CBHW071442300726
48976CB00004B/1421